Gloomy Louie

Gloomy Louie

Phyllis Green

Illustrated by John Wallner

Albert Whitman & Company, Chicago

J
G

For Bertha and Mickey

Library of Congress Cataloging in Publication Data

Green, Phyllis
  Gloomy Louie

  SUMMARY: Gloomy Louie begins to develop optimism
and self-confidence when he successfully handles
a crisis.
  [1. Self-reliance—Fiction. 2. Conduct of life
—Fiction] I. Wallner, John C. II. Title.
PZ7.G82615G1   [Fic]   79-28533
ISBN 0-8075-2962-1

Contents

1

Cactuses and Snakes

Louie Bix kicked open the door with his muddy baseball shoes. He threw his mitt on the hall rug. He dropped his bat in the umbrella stand. He sat on the stairway and held his head in his hands.

"I'm home," he groaned.

His big brother, Basil Jr., who everyone called Base, came running down the steps and leap-frogged over Louie.

"If it isn't old sad sack! How'd you do today?" Base asked.

"I struck out twice," Louie said, glumly.

"Well, put a smile on your face. Things have been happening here. We've been transferred. We're moving to Phoenix."

Louie looked up. "Transferred...Phoenix? That's in the desert. All that cactus? All those snakes?"

"You better believe it!" Base said.

Louie stood up and walked out to the kitchen.

"Hey Dad," he said. "Tell me we're not moving to Phoenix."

His father hung up the telephone and took the car keys from his pants pocket.

"Hi Louie! How's the old man?" he said. He patted Louie on the shoulder. "Listen, I'll be right back. I want to go out and get some champagne so Mom and I can celebrate."

"Dad, we're not moving to Phoenix. Are we?"

"Yes, we are, Louie," Mr. Bix said.

"But *why*?" Louie pleaded. "Did Mom get a promotion?"

"How do you like Joanna Bix, Vice President! How does that sound?" his father said, proudly.

"But I thought we would always live here in Michigan. It's nice here. I thought you would be my teacher next year. I thought..."

"Louie, let's talk about it when I get back, okay?" Mr. Bix opened the front door, then looked back at Louie. "Hey, who won the game?"

"I struck out twice," Louie said.

"Did you lose the game?" his father asked.

Louie looked at his muddy cleats. "My team won, 5-zip, but I struck out twice."

"Then you won!" his father said. He walked back and ruffled Louie's hair. "You won, you bum! Smile!"

"Well, sort of," Louie said, "but I struck out twice."

"Be back in five minutes," Mr. Bix said, "then we'll talk about Phoenix. You'll like it."

2

You Might Want to Get Some Cowboy Boots

Louie got the big pan out of the pan drawer. He took the Fun-to-Pop popcorn out of the food cupboard. He turned on the stove and melted the butter in the pan. He added the corn kernels. He placed the lid on top of the pan. He put on the pink hotpads that looked like mittens. He held the handles of the pan.

I think I'm going to be sick, he thought.

The kernels began to make popping noises. Louie shook the pan over the burner.

I don't want to move to Phoenix. I can't even spell Phoenix. It's going to make me sick to move to Phoenix.

The popping in the pan stopped. Louie turned off the stove and dumped the popcorn into a yellow bowl. He poured himself a glass of orange juice.

"I think I'm going to be sick," he said as he walked into the family room.

He sat down, turned on the TV, drank his orange juice, and ate the whole bowl of popcorn.

His father walked into the family room, carrying a bottle of champagne.

"I'm back," Mr. Bix said. He looked at a few burned popcorn kernels in the bottom of the yellow bowl. "You're going to be sick!" he said to Louie.

"How did you know?" Louie asked.

"Do you want to talk now?"

Louie nodded.

"Then turn off the TV."

Louie got up and turned off the set.

"This is a wonderful opportunity for Mom, Louie," his father said. "We have six weeks before we move, so you'll finish school here and have three weeks of Michigan summer. I think you'll like Phoenix. It's in the state of Arizona. Arizona is quite different from Michigan."

"But I like Michigan," Louie said.

"Of course you do. We all do. But we will like Arizona, too. Arizona is hot and dry. There is a lot of cactus. And a lot of desert. It snows in Arizona, sometimes. There isn't much grass. There are mostly cactuses and palm trees and swimming pools and horses. There are real cowboys and real Indians in Arizona."

"Real ones? Really?" Louie asked. "I'll probably get caught in a gunfight and die."

"You've been watching too many old movies, Louie."

"It sounds dangerous there."

"You might want to get a pair of cowboy boots. Base wants to get a pair and so do I."

"Do you expect me to ride a wild horse? Do you want me to be bitten by a rattlesnake?"

"The Grand Canyon is in Arizona. We can go see it and ride down into the canyon on burros."

"Not me! No thanks," Louie said. "I'd get the first clumsy burro in the history of the Grand Canyon. It would make a false step, trip over its nose, turn two flip-flops, and I'd be sailing to the bottom of the canyon at six hundred miles an hour."

"You'll like the Grand Canyon, Louie," his father said.

"I don't feel I will," Louie said.

Mr. Bix began to eat the burned kernels in the bottom of the yellow bowl. "It won't be easy moving to a new place," he told Louie. "We'll have to leave good friends behind. We'll have to leave a good ice-cream store and a dentist who doesn't hurt us when he

cleans our teeth and a lake where we can always catch a good perch. We're going to have to leave the best pizza restaurant in America, here in Detroit. But you see, Louie, we're going to be hopeful. Maybe we'll find the best taco restaurant in Phoenix! Maybe we'll find the best friends we've ever had in Phoenix. Maybe Phoenix has the best bicycle trails in the world. Maybe we'll find a piece of gold in the desert. Maybe the best part of our lives will happen in Phoenix."

Louie frowned and shook his head.

"And our family will be together. That's the important thing," his father said. "We'll help each other to be happy. We'll help each other to find friends. And we'll remember Michigan, together."

"I think I'm going to be sick," Louie said.

"I'm not surprised, after all that popcorn," his father said. "Well, I'll put the champagne for your mother on ice. Hey now, Louie, chin up. You're going to like Phoenix.

15

And how about a smile for Mom, when she gets home. A smile on your face would make Mom so happy."

Mr. Bix gave Louie a hug. Then he went to the kitchen.

"I don't think I can take this," Louie said.

He walked outside and leaned against his father's blue station wagon. "Boy, is this car old and rusty and cruddy! It'll never make it to Phoenix."

Louie walked to the back of the car and wrote in the dirt with his finger, "Nix on Feenix."

Mrs. Bix pulled her old white convertible into the driveway.

"Hi, honey," she said, waving.

Louie remembered what his father had said. Louie should smile to make his mother feel good. Something wonderful had happened to her, and the whole family should be glad.

Louie put his lips together and tried to

move them into a big smile. His cheeks felt like concrete. He tried very hard to push the corners of his mouth up. He felt his eyes bulge. He thought he must look like a chimpanzee with a headache.

His mother hugged him. "Oh Louie, this is the best day of my life," she said, laughing.

They walked into the house together.

3

That's the Way
the Cookie Crumbles

The next day Louie went to cut the grass at Mrs. Calaban's house, two blocks away from where his family lived. He rang her bell for almost five minutes before she answered it.

"Oh! Look who it is," she said when she opened the door.

"Shall I cut the grass?" Louie said.

"I'm existing," Mrs. Calaban said. "Of course, I'll never get over Mr. Calaban. Time doesn't help. Not a bit."

"You'll have to get another person to cut the grass after July 15. My mom's been transferred to Phoenix, Arizona," Louie said. "I thought my dad would be my teacher next year. But he called the schools in Phoenix, and they have an opening in first grade. He's going to teach first grade, and I thought he was going to teach fifth grade next year. They keep saying I'll like Phoenix, but I don't think so."

Mrs. Calaban came out and sat down on the front porch. "The days are all the same to me. I get through them."

"Your grass is pretty high," Louie said.

"Three years. Time doesn't help," she said.

"SHALL I CUT THE GRASS?" Louie said.

"No need to shout, young man. If you look right at me and speak clearly, I can hear you."

"Do you want me to cut the grass today?"

"Oh, do you like it?" Mrs. Calaban said,

19

smoothing her dress. "I got it at Hudson's. It wasn't on sale."

Louie decided to get the lawnmower. He waved and walked off the porch.

"Why don't you cut the grass before you go?" Mrs. Calaban called.

Louie nodded his head up and down to let her know he would. He got the lawnmower out of Mrs. Calaban's garage. There seemed to be enough gas. The motor started on his second try. It usually took twenty minutes to get going.

This must be my lucky day, Louie thought.

He began to mow the part of Mrs. Calaban's lawn between the street and the sidewalk. As he mowed, he tried not to think about his best friend, Chubby, and what Chubby had said about Phoenix. But he couldn't help it. Chubby and Louie had been best friends ever since they were babies. Chubby's name was really Earl. Chubby was not chubby. He was fat. Sometimes people called Louie and Chubby, Laurel and Hardy.

Chubby had said it was great that Louie was moving to Phoenix.

"How can you say that?" Louie had said. "I'm your best friend. You won't ever see me again."

"That's the way it is today," Chubby had answered. "People move all over the place. Remember Mike Pepples, Deborah Stick, Timmy Wortworth? They all moved away. That's the way it is. Then new kids move here."

"But I'm ME," Louie had said. "You'll miss ME."

"That's the way the cookie crumbles," Chubby had said, crumbling the chocolate chip cookie in his fist and dribbling the crumbs onto his desk.

"You're heartless," Louie had moaned.

"You'll live," Chubby had said, licking the last cookie crumbs from his fingers.

Louie mowed around Mrs. Calaban's silver maple tree. *Just my luck to get a heartless best friend,* he said to himself. *I should have known.* He mowed around Mrs. Calaban's pine trees, all in a row. *There probably won't be any lawns to mow in Phoenix. Just pebbles and dirt. How will I earn money? I'll go broke. I'll be the first bankrupt kid in the West.*

4

If Dad Was My Teacher

When Louie finished cutting Mrs. Calaban's grass, he went home and found his mother in the kitchen, making dinner.

"Hi, Ms. Vice President," he said.

His mother laughed. "Feel free to call me just Ms. Mom," she said.

"What are you doing?" Louie asked.

"Don't say a word," Mrs. Bix said. "I know your dad makes better lasagna than I do, but we traded nights to cook so you're stuck with mine."

"Ick," Louie said.

"Look, I'm not so hot at lasagna, but I sew on a great button."

"The only thing is, we don't have to eat Dad's buttons," Louie said.

"Okay, so I'm a rotten cook. Do you want to sue me? On second thought, why don't you help? There are too many things to do with lasagna."

Louie stared at her. "I guess this means I'll have to wash my hands."

His mother looked in the cookbook. "Hmmm-n. I've got to admit I don't see grass cuttings in the ingredients."

"I might have known," Louie said, going to the sink and grabbing the soap.

His mother studied the cookbook. She murmured, "I never can remember if the meat sauce goes in before the mozzarella or if the noodles go between the cottage cheese and Parmesan or... Maybe we should go out for dinner."

Louie dried his hands. "Here, let me," he

said to his mother as he took the cookbook
out of her hands.

He carefully drained the lasagna
noodles and laid them in the bottom of the
big baking pan.

"There are scorpions and Gila monsters
in Arizona. You can get lost in the desert. It's
hot there. I mean really hot," he said.

"There are palm trees, too," his mother
said. "Dad thinks we should get a house with
a swimming pool."

"I suppose you'll force me to go down into the Grand Canyon on a burro. I'll probably get the clumsy one," Louie said.

"Should I pour the meat sauce now?" his mother asked.

Louie nodded yes.

"Dad was going to be my teacher next year."

Mrs. Bix put down the pan. She hugged Louie. "I know. That would have been such fun, wouldn't it?"

"I still hadn't decided if I would call him Dad or Mr. Bix or..."

"Or Hey-you," his mother said.

"Yeah," Louie said.

"Forty-five minutes in the oven?" his mother asked.

"How can you know all about computers and nothing about cooking? Thirty minutes in the oven. Fifteen out of the oven, before we can eat. I'll probably get dehydrated our first day in Phoenix."

"I'm sorry you're unhappy, Louie."

Louie shrugged his shoulders. "That's the story of my life," he said.

His mother put the lasagna in the oven. Louie went into the family room to wait for dinner. He threw himself down on the plaid sofa, even though he knew he was not supposed to. His parents always said, "The sofa is not a jungle gym."

Oh boy, he thought, *I really wanted Dad to be my teacher. If he was my teacher, I could get all A's. And I wouldn't have to sit down if I missed a word in a spelling bee. And I could be first out the door for recess and could clean the blackboard erasers all the time. And I'd never have to be field trip partner with Marsha Mudge, ever. And I wouldn't be sent to the principal's office if I got into trouble. Not if Dad was my teacher next year.*

"I think I'm going to hate Phoenix," Louie said out loud. "I really think I am."

"Dinner!" his mother called.

"I'm pretty sure I'm going to hate it,"

Louie said, as he walked back into the kitchen.

"Don't be silly," his mother said. "You love lasagna."

5

The Strike-Out King

On Saturday the whole family went to see Louie's baseball game. He warned them, "Don't watch me when I'm up to bat. You'll only get depressed."

Louie sat on the bench for the first inning. He batted in the second. He swung a few bats wildly in the air before deciding, as he usually did, to use his own.

He tapped the batting helmet and thought, *This is the day I'll get hit on the head, the day when all the doctors are on vacation.* He stepped into the batter's box. He tapped home plate with his bat and moved his feet into place. He cut the air a few times with his bat. He knew he would hit a home run if he could just connect with the ball.

The umpire yelled, "Batter up."

The lump in Louie's throat felt as big as a baseball. *Please, please,* he thought, *let me get a hit.*

He watched the pitcher wind up, and he saw the ball leave the pitcher's hand.

"Steee-rike!" the umpire called.

I'll swing at the next ball, Louie thought, *even if it comes rolling on the ground.*

The second pitch was high and wide. Louie didn't swing at it. The umpire called, "Ball one."

Louie really pulled the bat around on the third pitch but only fanned the air.

"Steee-rike two," the umpire called.

Louie thought he was going to hook into the next ball. He swung and felt nothing. The ball thudded into the catcher's mitt.

"Steee-rike three. You're out," the umpire called.

Louie went back to sit on the bench. *That's the story of my life,* he thought.

The coach put him in to play center field before the end of the second inning. But no hits reached center field, so Louie just stood there. He went back to sit on the bench at the end of the inning and only came up to bat again in the sixth. When he stepped up to the batter's box, his team was ahead, 2-1.

The pitcher's first ball hit Louie in the left ankle. He got a walk and limped to first base. But his team struck out before he got any farther. At the end of the game, they had won, 2-1.

Louie walked home with Base and his parents.

"Boy, does my ankle hurt," Louie said. "I'll probably lose my foot."

"You won again," Base said. "You're on a great team."

"I'm their strike-out king," Louie said.

"You can't be," Base said. "You play center field. Only a pitcher can be strike-out king. That's what a pitcher is when he strikes everybody out."

"No. That's what *I* am. When all you do is strike out, you've just got to be strike-out king. Did you ever hear of anyone else with a .000 batting average?"

Base shook his head. "I never heard of a loser on a winning team till I met you. You're the gloomiest kid I ever saw. You know what kind of king you are? You're the Doom King."

Mr. Bix said, "Hey Louie, Mom and I were just thinking about something. Your team has a great win record. You just might win the pennant. Mom says if you do, she'll arrange a business trip so you and she can fly back for the pennant banquet dinner. How does that sound?"

"You mean you'll make me get on an airplane?" Louie said.

6

What If I Don't Find a Friend?

After dinner, Louie was in his room. He saw Base go past his door.

"Oh, Base," he said.

Base stopped and looked in at Louie.

"Hi, Doom," Base said.

"I think I'm getting a stomach-ache, Base," Louie said.

"Tell Mom," Base said. "She's in charge of stomach-aches. I hate it when little kids throw up."

"I'm not going to throw up," Louie said. "It's Phoenix in my stomach. Phoenix makes my stomach ache."

Base came into Louie's room and sat down. "Where's that poster I gave you?"

"The one of the movie star? I can't hang that poster in here. I'm too young. Grandma would have a fit."

Base laughed. "Oh, Doom, you think of everything," he said.

"I don't know how to make friends," Louie said. "I never had to learn. I've known Chubby since I was a baby. I'm scared, Base. How will I ever make friends? I can't go up to a baby in Phoenix and ask it to be my best friend."

"You'll make friends in school," Base said.

"How?"

"Or you'll see a kid ride his bike past our new house and you'll call out to him, 'where'd you get that crate, in the junkyard?' "

"No, I'll say something stupid like 'that's

a real nice bike you got there.' I know I'll do it wrong. You'll be mortified with me, Base. I'll be the only kid in Phoenix that doesn't have a friend."

"I'll get my friend's little brother to play with you," Base said.

"You will?"

"Sure."

"Who is your friend?"

"I don't know yet. But when I get there, I'll get a friend," Base said.

"But what if he doesn't have a little brother?" Louie said.

"Then he won't be my friend," Base said.

"Yeah?"

"Yeah."

"You're nice, Base," Louie said.

"You think *you* feel funny," Base said. "Just imagine how Dad feels."

"What do you mean?" Louie said. "Dad loves the idea of Phoenix. He can't wait to walk around in cowboy boots. He's practicing standing bow-legged."

"I picked him up at school the other day, and I heard some of the other teachers teasing him."

"Yeah? What about?" Louie asked.

"About Mom making more money than he does."

"Does she?"

"Of course she does. They don't pay school teachers anything. Didn't you know that? And how do you think Dad feels about changing schools? He likes the school he's in. Now he's got to go to Phoenix and teach babies."

"I know. He was going to teach me. Now he's got to teach first-graders. But Dad never complained to me," Louie said.

"Because he doesn't only think of himself," Base said. "That's why. Because he's a nice guy and he looks for the best in every situation."

"Don't you think I try to do that?" Louie asked. "Don't you? Don't you think I try and try?"

"Did it ever occur to you that I might like to graduate with the kids I've known all my life? That I might miss Freddy and Mary Lou? Did it ever occur to you that every time I see Mary Lou she cries her eyes out?"

"She does?" Louie said.

"Or that Mom might be nervous, wondering how the people in the new office will like her? Or scared of all the traveling she'll be doing in her new job?"

"Mom is scared, too?" Louie said. He scratched his head. "Base, if no one wants to move, why are we?"

"Because this is Mom's chance," Base said. "You'll understand when you grow up." He started to leave, but he turned back to Louie and smiled. "I'll be your best friend in Phoenix until you find someone your age to play with. Then you can tell me to go back to just being your brother."

Louie ran to Base and hugged him.

"I know how it is," Base said. He patted Louie's shoulder.

7

Schools Shouldn't
Make Kids Take P.E.

The next Tuesday when Louie went to cut Mrs. Calaban's grass, he had a terrible time getting her to answer the door. He rang the bell. He knocked. He called. But she didn't answer. He walked around to the back door. He pounded on it and called Mrs. Calaban's name as loud as he could. Finally she came to the back door.

"Well, look who it is," she said.

Louie was out of breath. "I've been

calling you and calling you. I was worried about you," he puffed.

"You naughty boy," Mrs. Calaban said. "You didn't mention you were moving. I talked to your mother on the phone last night. She says she's dragging your whole family off to Phoenix. What's the matter with Michigan, I'd like to know? Your father ought to lay down the law with her. We have pants suits to thank for this."

"Do you want me to cut your grass?" Louie asked.

"I don't suppose your mother gave one thought to me when she decided to drag you all away. Nobody thinks about this big lawn I have to take care of all by myself."

Louie had a notebook and pencil in his pocket. He took it out and wrote, "Do you want your grass cut?" He showed the note to Mrs. Calaban.

"Of course I want my grass cut, Louie. You don't have to write messages. Just look at me and speak clearly," Mrs. Calaban said.

Louie nodded and went to cut the grass.

The lawnmower started on the first try.
Just my luck, Louie thought, *this lawnmower
begins to work right when I'm moving away.*

He began to mow the lawn around the
row of pine trees. He could have mowed the
lawn the same way all the time, but he was
afraid he'd get bored, so he always had a
different system. Sometimes he mowed in a
straight line, and sometimes he mowed in

wavy rows. Sometimes he mowed in square patches. Once he mowed his last name, *Bix,* in Mrs. Calaban's backyard. But before she saw it, he had mowed the rest of the grass and the *Bix* had disappeared.

Louie had been mowing Mrs. Calaban's yard for a year and a half. Base had begun mowing it, back when Mr. Calaban's heart had gotten bad, but Mr. Calaban had died, anyway. Last summer, Base had given the job to Louie.

Mrs. Calaban couldn't forget Mr. Calaban. She talked about him all the time. Louie had already forgotten what Mr. Calaban's face looked like. He could only remember that Mr. Calaban wore black glasses. Sometimes Louie tried to remember if Mrs. Calaban had been a happy person when Mr. Calaban was alive. She'd always said she was happy then, but Louie couldn't remember if she was or not. Her hearing had been better then. Louie knew her hearing was getting worse. He felt sorry for Mrs.

Calaban. He was sorry she couldn't hear and sorry she'd lost her husband.

Maybe I could get Chubby to mow Mrs. Calaban's grass, Louie thought. But he knew that wasn't a good idea. Chubby didn't like to do anything that required physical activity. He didn't play baseball or football. He just read and watched TV and wrote letters to his senator that began, "Schools shouldn't make kids take physical education." He went to a lot of movies, too. When Chubby grew up he wanted to collect old movies and make people pay to see them. Louie had always planned to make the popcorn and sell it to the people who paid to see Chubby's old movies. But he guessed moving to Phoenix would end those plans.

Louie mowed around the silver maple tree.

"I'll miss you, you dumb, stupid tree," he whispered. "If you don't get your trunk out of the way I'm going to kick it."

Louie waited.

"This is your last chance."

The tree did not move.

Louie kicked the trunk. "You dumb tree," he said. "Why don't *you* move!"

8

Hiccup!

It was hot Tuesday night, and Louie had trouble going to sleep. He decided he was thirsty. On his way to the bathroom, he heard his parents talking in their bedroom. He would not have stopped to listen, but he thought he heard his mother say his name. He paused by their door to make sure.

"...makes everything into a calamity," his mother said.

"Nothing is ever right," his father said.

"Bzzz...bzzz...life can be so beautiful!

45

Not for bzzz...unhappy...bzzz...depressing...bzzz...no fun at all."

"A real drag," his father said. "A real loser."

Louie wanted to melt away. *That's me,* he thought. *They're talking about me!*

He felt a hiccup coming on. *Don't let me hiccup,* he thought.

"HIC-CUP."

"Who's there?" his father demanded.

"Me," Louie said softly.

"Louie, is that you? Are you sick? Come in here," his mother said.

He walked slowly into the room.

"Do you have a sore throat?" his mother said.

"I'm okay. I just need a drink of water."

"Louie, did you hear what your mother and I were talking about?" his father asked.

"HIC-CUP. Excuse me. No. I mean, a little. I just heard a little...practically nothing," Louie said, not looking at his father.

"Well, just remember the family rule. We don't repeat things. We wouldn't want Leslie Calaban to know we were discussing her."

"Were you talking about Mrs. Calaban?" Louie blurted out. "*Mrs. Calaban?*"

"Who did you think we were talking about?"

"Oh," Louie said, smiling. "I didn't know. HIC-CUP."

"Get your drink of water, honey," his mother said.

"Okay."

Louie got a drink of water. His hiccups stopped. He walked back to bed, past his parents' room. They weren't talking anymore. He guessed they were sleeping.

Boy am I dumb, he thought, *to have imagined they were talking about me.*

But, really, he knew he was kidding himself. He knew the very words his parents had used to describe Leslie Calaban could be used perfectly to describe Louie Bix. He *was* depressing, unhappy—a loser. He was a real drag.

I'm the biggest drag I know, Louie thought. *How does anybody stand me? How do I stand myself? Base is right to call me Doom. I've never had a happy thought in my life. I don't know how to think happy.*

Louie went to sleep trying to figure out how to be a happy person. How could he be happy about baseball...about Phoenix... about anything?

9

Puffs of Smoke!

Two days later Louie's team won another ball game, 7-3. Louie played center field for three innings. He caught one pop fly. But he struck out both times he came to bat.

He walked home swinging his bat at trees and fences and mosquitoes. As he passed Mrs. Calaban's corner he saw puffs of smoke. He sniffed the air, and it smelled like fire.

He decided to check. He rang Mrs.

Calaban's bell. She didn't answer. He walked around to her back door, and then he just stared. Black smoke was coming out of Mrs. Calaban's kitchen windows!

"Mrs. Calaban!" he screamed.

He ran to the house next door. He rang the bell and pounded on the door.

"Help! Fire! Call the fire company."

But no one answered that door, either.

Oh no, Louie thought.

He ran back to Mrs. Calaban's front door. "Mrs. Calaban, open up! Your house is on fire!" he yelled.

A car turned the corner. Louie ran out to the street and flagged it down. The driver was a boy Base knew from high school.

"This house is on fire," Louie said. "Can you get the cops and the fire trucks?"

The boy said he would and sped off.

"Oh!" Louie shouted. "Oh, Mrs. Calaban, you've got to answer the door."

He pounded and yelled. He hit the door with his bat.

"You've got to hear me, Mrs. Calaban."

He whirled around and saw the picture window. He put his face up to the glass.

"Mrs. Calaban! Can you hear me?"

She wasn't in the living room.

Louie ran to the dining-room window. Pushing the juniper bushes aside, he peered in.

"Mrs. Calaban!"

She wasn't in the dining room.

"Please, Mrs. Calaban, where are you?"

He ran to the side of the house. His shirt tore as he climbed through the rose bushes. He looked in the bedroom window. Mrs. Calaban was on the bed.

"I found you!" Louie shouted.

She lay still.

He tried to open the window, but it was locked. He lifted his bat and smashed the window. Glass flew everywhere. Carefully Louie reached inside and unlocked the window. Then he opened it and crawled into the room.

He ran over to Mrs. Calaban and tried to pick her up.

She opened her eyes. "Unhand me, you hooligan!" she ranted, tossing her arms about and knocking Louie to the floor.

He quickly jumped up.

"Your house is on fire!"

"I smell smoke," Mrs. Calaban said. "Louie Bix, how did you get in my house? I don't need my lawn cut today!"

Louie grabbed Mrs. Calaban's hand and pulled her to the bedroom window.

"Fire," Louie said carefully.

"Hair?" Mrs. Calaban asked, checking to see if hers was askew.

"Fire." He wrote it on the musty windowsill.

"What are we waiting for?" Mrs. Calaban said. "Let's go!"

They crawled out the bedroom window and landed in the rose bushes. Fire trucks and police cars came up the street as Louie and Mrs. Calaban emerged from the bushes.

They crossed the street, then stood on the sidewalk, arm in arm, and watched as the firemen began to hose water on the burning kitchen.

"Oh my, I thought I turned that burner off," Mrs. Calaban said. "I always double-check. I wonder. I had a cup of tea before my nap. But I always turn the burner off..."

Black smoke was still filtering out of Mrs. Calaban's kitchen windows.

"Everything will be ruined," Mrs. Calaban said. "Smoke damaged or water damaged. Ruined. Everything. Nothing saved. I have nothing. We should have saved something. We should have brought *something* out of the house."

Louie looked at Mrs. Calaban. "But we did," he said.

"What's that? Speak clearly," Mrs. Calaban said.

"We saved the most important thing in your house," Louie said.

"What's that? You saved something?

You say you saved something from my house? What is it? What is it? Let me see it," Mrs. Calaban demanded.

Louie looked at the house behind them. He ran up on the porch and asked the woman who lived there if he could borrow something. She went into the house and brought him back a hand mirror from her dresser.

Louie took the mirror to Mrs. Calaban. "Look," he said.

"What's this?" Mrs. Calaban said. "I never saw this before. This didn't come from my house. You said you saved the most important thing in my house. I never saw this mirror before in my life!"

Louie pointed to Mrs. Calaban's reflection in the mirror. Then he pointed to her face.

"You," he said. "You, you, you, you!"

"What do you mean?" Mrs. Calaban said quietly. "Me?"

Louie nodded.

"Me?"

"You, I saved YOU."

"Why Louie," Mrs. Calaban said, thoughtfully. "Sometimes I speak before I...oh, dear...Mr. Calaban used to say, 'Sometimes, Leslie, you complain before you think about what's important.' "

Mrs. Calaban talked to the firemen. They told her the kitchen was a mess but that everything else was okay. They said she should stay somewhere else until the house aired out.

Mrs. Calaban called her friend Mrs. Francken, who gladly invited her to spend a few days. Louie walked Mrs. Calaban over to Mrs. Francken's, three blocks west.

"Finally something horrible happened to me," Mrs. Calaban said. "All my life I've been waiting for something horrible to happen. And now it has."

"I think I saved her life," Louie said. "Me."

"What's that?" Mrs. Calaban said.

"I was talking to myself," Louie said.

"Just speak clearly," Mrs. Calaban said. "I'll hear you. Of course, things could have been *more* horrible. As you said, Louie, I could have died. I'm going to have to remember that."

"I never thought I could be brave," Louie said. "But I *was* brave, without even thinking about it. Maybe I'm kind of great. I almost feel like smiling. Wait till Base hears about this."

"Louie," Mrs. Calaban said, "I'm ashamed you had to point out to me that *I* was the most important thing in my house. That was so sweet of you, and, of course, you were right. I'm a very lucky woman today. And I'm going to try to live my life appreciating how lucky I am. I'm going to turn over a new leaf."

"I'm pretty important in my house, too," Louie said. "But there are four of us in our house. We're all important. I'm going to miss Michigan. But I'm going to try real hard in Phoenix. Old great me."

"Here we are," Mrs. Calaban said, stopping in front of Mrs. Francken's little blue ranch house. "Well, Louie," she said, "this was quite a day. It made me think."

"It made me think, too," Louie said.

"Yes, Ilsa Francken's lilacs do smell good," Mrs. Calaban said, her nose moving as she sniffed the white flowers.

"I said today made me think, too," Louie said.

"Goodbye, dear," Mrs. Calaban said. She waved as she walked up to Mrs. Francken's ranch house.

10

A Hungry Hero

Louie could hardly eat his dinner because he was talking so much.

"And then...she wasn't in the dining-room," he said, suspensefully.

"For Pete's sake, did you find her?" Base asked.

"So I turned..." Louie said dramatically, "afraid the worst had happened. I ran to the bedroom window. Thorns on the rose bushes tried to stop me, but nothing could stop me then."

"Will you cut it out?" Base said. "They already gave the Oscars this year."

"I looked in the bedroom, fearing the worst," Louie said.

"Louie, can we jump to the part where you either found or did not find Leslie Calaban?" his father asked.

"Yeah," Base said.

"I'd appreciate it, too," Mrs. Bix joined in.

"But I wanted to relive it," Louie said. "Oh well. Yes, I found her."

"Is she okay?"

"Yeah, she's fine," Louie said, taking a mouthful of applesauce.

"Was she in the bedroom?" Base asked.

"Boy, this chicken is good, Dad. What's the sauce on it?" Louie asked.

"It's a white sauce," his father said, "with a few chives for color."

60

"Dad! Louie!" Base said. "I want to know how you got her out of the house?"

Louie sighed. "Later, Base. I'm so hungry. Being a hero makes you hungry, you know."

"Mom!" Base said, pleading.

Mrs. Bix smiled at Base. "I'm sure our hero will go through the story from start to finish after he's eaten."

Louie held a drumstick out of his mouth long enough to say, "Yeah, Base, I'll probably tell you the story so many times you'll want to stuff cotton in your ears. I'll probably be telling it when I'm seventy-eight years old and you're..."

"Dead," Base said.

"You'll get to know every little detail," Louie said, "every second, every step."

"Eat your chicken," Mrs. Bix said, smiling.

After dessert, Louie's father said, "But what about your baseball game, Louie? You didn't tell us if you won."

Louie almost said, *I left my bat at Mrs. Calaban's house, that's the story of my life.* But he caught himself just in time. "My team, I mean, we won!" he said. "Yeah, we won another game. Isn't it boring? We win all the time!"

"Hey, that's great!" Base said.

"Yeah. We won!" Louie said. A smile began on his lips and grew across his face. "You know what, Base? I caught a pop fly. I really did! You should have seen me catch it. Man, I aimed for it and grabbed it and held on like anything. It felt like it was glued to my glove! I tell you, that kid was out. I really got him out. It was the first out in the fourth inning and I did it."

"That's wonderful, Louie," his mother said.

"Yeah, we'll probably win the pennant, all right," Louie said.

"I could still arrange that business trip. We could fly back for the banquet. You could see your old friends. Think about it," his mother said.

"I'll think about it," Louie said, nodding. "It might be fun, you know?"